Honeypot Hill

Saffron Thimble's
Sewing Shop

To the City

The Orchards

Paddle Steamer
Quay

Aunt
Marigold's
General
Store

Lavender Valley
Garden Centre

Healing House and Garden

Lavender Lake

The Worthingtons' House

Bumble Bee's Teashop

Lavender Lake
School of Dance

Hedgerows Hotel
Where Mimosa lives

SCHOOL

Peppermint
Pond

Rosehip School

Summer Meadow

Christmas Corner

Wildspice Woods

Honeysuckle Cottage
Poppy's House

Forget-Me-Not Cottage
Grandpa's House and Office

Poppy Field

N
W E
S

Honeypot Cottage
Honey and Granny Bumble's House

Blossom
Bakehouse

Cornsilk Castle
and Courtyard

Village Hall

Sage's
Vet Surgery

Post Office

River Swan

Beehive
Beauty Salon

Barley Farm
The Meadowsweets' House

Riverside
Stables

Honeypot Hill
Railway Station

To Camomile Cove
via Periwinkle Lane

TWINKLETOES
A PICTURE CORGI BOOK: 978 0 552 55662 0

First published in Great Britain in 2006 by Picture Corgi,
an imprint of Random House Children's Books

This edition published 2007

5 7 9 10 8 6

Picture Corgi Books are published by Random House Children's Books, Sydney,
Auckland, Johannesburg, New Delhi and agencies throughout the world.

THE RANDOM HOUSE GROUP Limited Reg. No. 954009
www.kidsatrandomhouse.co.uk
www.princesspoppy.com

A CIP catalogue record for this book is available from the British Library.

Printed in China

Princess Poppy

Twinkletoes

Written by Janey Louise Jones

PICTURE CORGI

"I wish *I* had a rocking horse like Apple Blossom," said Poppy as she stood in Honey's playroom, brushing the horse's thick white mane.

"Yeah, but it would be even better to have a *real* pony, wouldn't it?" said Honey.

"My cousin Daisy has a *real* pony," announced Poppy. "He's called Parsley and she keeps him at Riverside Stables. She's *so* lucky."

"I know, let's see if Granny Bumble will take us to Riverside Stables to see some real ponies," suggested Honey.

As they arrived at the stables on Barley Farm, they saw David Sage, the Honeypot Hill vet.

"Hello everyone!" he said as he walked towards them, gently leading a small chestnut pony.

"Aw, that pony is *soooooooo* sweet!" cried Poppy. "Who does he belong to?"

"Well, no one really," explained David. "I got a call from Farmer Meadowsweet asking me to rescue a pony from the hillside. I think he must have got lost up there, poor thing. He's very weak, and hungry and thirsty too. Because of his white feet we've called him Twinkletoes."

"Can we ride him?" chorused Poppy and Honey. "Pleeease?"

"Oh girls, I would love to say yes, but I'm afraid
Twinkletoes is just not well enough at the moment.
He needs lots of fresh food, water, medicine
and rest before he can be ridden."

"Maybe we could help to make him better, and *then* we would be able to ride him, wouldn't we?" said Poppy.

"Great idea, girls, and I'm sure Daisy will show you what to do," smiled David.

Just then, Daisy came trotting over on her pony, Parsley.

"Hi, Poppy!" called Daisy. "Are you here to learn how to be a Pony Princess?"

"Well, sort of. Granny Bumble brought us here to see some real ponies. We've just met Twinkletoes, but he's not well and needs lots of looking after," said Poppy.

"Let's go over to the stables," suggested Daisy.

"I'll show you how to care for a pony. I'm sure Twinkletoes will get better soon if we look after him properly. You'll need to groom him, gently, like this," Daisy explained to the younger girls.

"Every day he'll need a
net filled with hay and
a bucket of fresh water . . .

. . . a clean bed of straw,

and maybe give him the
odd apple or sugar lump
as a treat," said Daisy.

"I think Twinkletoes will get well really soon because his stable is so snuggly and we know just how to look after him now," Poppy said as they kissed him goodbye.

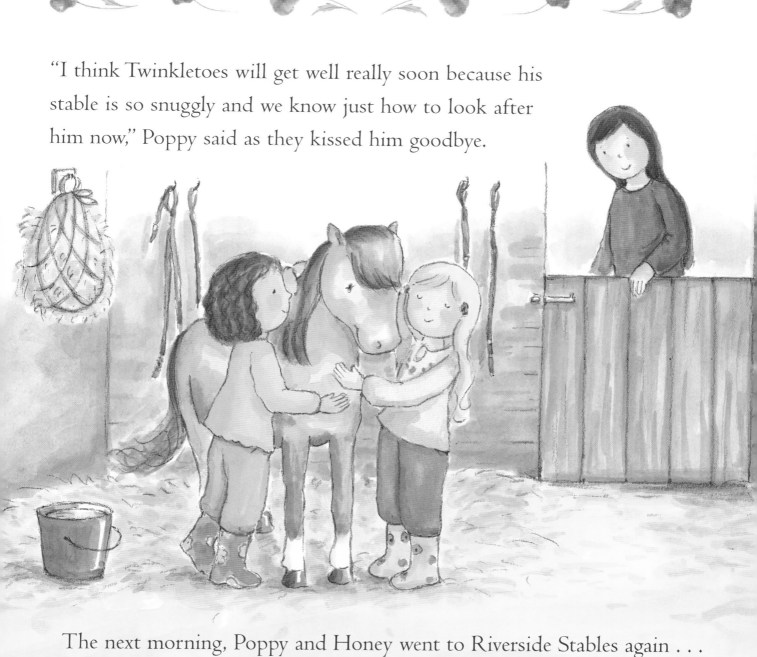

The next morning, Poppy and Honey went to Riverside Stables again . . .

Twinkletoes was happy to see them. Honey gave him an apple, holding her hand flat like Daisy had shown them, and he looked even happier.

"Hi, you two," called Daisy as she trotted past, "I'm off to the paddock to practise – I've got a show at the weekend. Do you want to watch?"

"Yes please, but we have to finish grooming Twinkletoes," said Poppy.

In the paddock, Daisy looked so confident as she jumped
Parsley over little wooden fences.

"Wow! I wish I could do that," sighed Poppy, "but I've
never even *been* on a pony. I'll *never* be as good as Daisy."

"I'll teach you to ride as soon as Twinkletoes is well enough —
if your mums let you!" Daisy said as she trotted past.

"Mum, can I have riding lessons?" asked Poppy as they sat down to supper. "I want to be as good as Daisy! She said she'd teach me."

"We'll see. But you'll have to wait until Twinkletoes is strong enough," explained Mum.

"Me and Honey have been looking after him for *ages* now. I don't think he's *ever* going to get better," moaned Poppy.

"You have to be patient, sweetheart, just like when you're ill and I take care of you. He'll soon be better, you'll see," said Mum softly.

Poppy and Honey were at the stables bright and early the next morning, desperately hoping that today would be the day.

"Hi David," said Poppy, "how's Twinkletoes? Can we ride him yet?"

"I'm sorry, he's still not ready," explained David. "I promise you won't have to wait much longer. You're both doing a great job — thank you for all your help."

Poppy smiled, but inside she was really cross. They had fed Twinkletoes. They had watered him and groomed him. They had kissed and cuddled him and even given him treats. And *still* he wasn't ready. It wasn't fair.

"Maybe we could ride another pony," suggested Honey.

"But I want to ride Twinkletoes," said Poppy. "He's *our* special pony."

"Yeah, you're right," Honey agreed. "Let's go and see how he is."

The next day, Poppy and Honey dragged their feet all the way
to the stables quite sure that today would be just the same.
As they arrived, Daisy came over, smiling broadly.

"Hi you two!" she called. "I've got a surprise for you —
back in a minute . . ."

Poppy and Honey thought they probably knew what it was,
but they didn't want to get their hopes up too much.

They peeped into Twinkletoes' stable, but he wasn't there,

so they dashed over to the paddock . . .

There he was, looking very smart in his bridle and saddle.
David was leading Twinkletoes towards them.

"Today's the day!" said Daisy, nearly as excited as her cousin and Honey.
"Hurray!" yelled Poppy as she and Honey raced over to Twinkletoes.

"I've got another surprise for you two," said Daisy.
"Come with me to the stable block . . ."

As the girls entered the stable block, they spotted two sets of beautiful riding clothes that Daisy had grown out of. They changed into jodhpurs, riding jackets with velvet collars, and shiny black boots.

"And choose a hat!" said Daisy, pointing to rows of little wooden shelves, each containing hard hats in black, brown and navy blue.

When they arrived back at the paddock, Mum and Granny Bumble were there too, and everyone told Poppy and Honey how smart they looked.

Daisy held Twinkletoes, while David helped Poppy into the saddle. Then Daisy led them round the paddock, with Poppy holding tightly onto the reins.

"Can we trot and then can we try some jumps?" pleaded Poppy.

"This is *only* your first lesson!" laughed Daisy. "You'll need a few more before we try anything too fancy."

Poppy didn't want the lesson to end, but Honey had worked really hard to make Twinkletoes better as well, so it *was* her turn.

"You are a perfect little princess — you didn't give up," said Mum. "Well done for looking after Twinkletoes, you and Honey have worked so hard."

"Thanks, Mum! I'll always take care of him, I promise," said Poppy, "especially since Daisy said she'd teach me how to do jumps. Can I please have another riding lesson tomorrow?"

"Yes, of course, now go to sleep my little Pony Princess. Sweet dreams!"